A Note to Parents and Caregivers:

Read-it! Readers are for children who are just starting on the amazing road to reading. These beautiful books support both the acquisition of reading skills and the love of books.

The PURPLE LEVEL presents basic topics and objects using high frequency words and simple language patterns.

The RED LEVEL presents familiar topics using common words and repeating sentence patterns.

The BLUE LEVEL presents new ideas using a larger vocabulary and varied sentence structure.

The YELLOW LEVEL presents more challenging ideas, a broad vocabulary, and wide variety in sentence structure.

The GREEN LEVEL presents more complex ideas, an extended vocabulary range, and expanded language structures.

The ORANGE LEVEL presents a wide range of ideas and concepts using challenging vocabulary and complex language structures.

When sharing a book with your child, read in short stretches, pausing often to talk about the pictures. Have your child turn the pages and point to the pictures and familiar words. And be sure to reread favorite stories or parts of stories.

There is no right or wrong way to share books with children. Find time to read with your child, and pass on the legacy of literacy.

Adria F. Klein, Ph.D.
Professor Emeritus
California State University
San Bernardino, California

Editor: Jill Kalz
Designer: Lori Bye
Page Production: Melissa Kes
Art Director: Nathan Gassman
Associate Managing Editor: Christianne Jones
The illustrations in this book were created with watercolor and ink.

Picture Window Books
151 Good Counsel Drive
P.O. Box 669
Mankato, MN 56002-0669
877-845-8392
www.picturewindowbooks.com

Printed in the United States of America.

All books published by Picture Window Books
are manufactured with paper containing at least
10 percent post-consumer waste.

Library of Congress Cataloging-in-Publication Data
Loewen, Nancy, 1964-
Lady Lulu liked to litter / by Nancy Loewen ; illustrated by Anna Kaiser.
p. cm. — (Read-it! readers: tongue twisters)
ISBN-13: 978-1-4048-4884-9 (library binding)
[1. Tongue twisters—Fiction. 2. Litter (Trash)—Fiction.] I. Kaiser, Anna, ill.
II. Title.
PZ7.L8268Lad 2008
[E]—dc22   2008006338

Lady Lulu
Liked to Litter

by Nancy Loewen
illustrated by Anna Kaiser

Special thanks to our reading adviser:

Adria F. Klein, Ph.D.
Professor Emeritus, California State University
San Bernardino, California

PICTURE WINDOW BOOKS
Minneapolis, Minnesota

Lady Lulu liked to litter.

She littered letters. She littered lids. She littered lemons and limes. Her loads of leftovers soon filled the lawn.

The people of Lucky Landing did not like Lady Lulu's littering. They thought Lady Lulu's litter would swallow up their village.

Lady Lulu's sister hoped to help. "Lulu," said Lady Liz. "Your littering is lazy. It is out of control! Lucky Landing has lots of proper places to put your locks, clocks, and lollipops."

But Lady Lulu didn't listen. "Silly Lizzy," she laughed. "Rules are for fools. They don't apply to me!"

Lady Lulu's brother gave her a long look. "Lulu," Lord Leo said. "Littering is lazy. Littering lacks style. Plus, it's against the law! Lucky Landing has lots of proper places to put your shells, bells, and balls."

But Lady Lulu didn't listen. She stuck her fingers in her ears. She called, "La-la-la-la-la!"

Lady Lulu went on littering. She littered plates and pails. She littered laundry and leaves. Soon Lady Lulu's loads of leftovers flooded the lake. They spilled onto the hill.

The people of Lucky Landing were filled with ill will. "Quit your littering!" they told Lady Lulu. "See the light! Get a clue!"

But Lady Lulu didn't listen. "Rules are dull," she said.

She plucked a piece of lint from her collar. It floated for a while. Then the loose lint landed on Lulu's litter pile.

And that's when it happened. Lady Lulu's litter started to slip. It started to slide. All of her leftovers came tumbling by her side. It was a litter landslide!

Everyone leaped away. Lady Lulu was alone.

"Help me!" Lady Lulu yelled from the middle of the litter. But the people of Lucky Landing didn't listen.

So Lady Lulu crawled over letters and lids. She climbed over lemons and limes.

She rolled over lumber, laundry, and lunches.

Finally, Lady Lulu faced the people.

"I've been a fool," she said. "I've been as stubborn as a mule! Lucky Landing has lots of proper places to put my logs, lists, and lutes. From now on, that's what I'll do, or my name isn't Lady Lulu!"

21

The people clapped loudly. Everyone was thrilled. "Lady Lulu no longer litters!" they yelled.

Then someone tossed Lady Lulu the clean-up bill.

More *Read-it!* Readers

Bright pictures and fun stories help you practice your reading skills. Look for more books at your level.

Alex and the Team Jersey

Alex and Toolie

Another Pet

Betty and Baxter's Batter Battle

The Big Pig

Bliss, Blueberries, and the Butterfly

Camden's Game

Cass the Monkey

Charlie's Tasks

Harold Hickok Had the Hiccups

Kyle's Recess

Marconi the Wizard

Peppy, Patch, and the Bath

Peter's Secret

Pets on Vacation

The Princess and the Tower

Sausages!

Theodore the Millipede

The Three Princesses

Tromso the Troll

Willie the Whale

The Zoo Band

On the Web

FactHound offers a safe, fun way to find Web sites related to topics in this book. All of the sites on FactHound have been researched by our staff.

1. Visit *www.facthound.com*

2. Type in this special code:
   1404848843

3. Click on the FETCH IT button.

Your trusty FactHound will fetch the best sites for you!
A complete list of *Read-it!* Readers is available on our Web site:
www.picturewindowbooks.com